Lucy
and the
Firestone

Written by June Crebbin

Illustrated by Polly Dunbar

WALKER BOOKS
AND SUBSIDIARIES

LONDON · BOSTON · SYDNEY · AUCKLAND

Over the hills and far away, a piece of land stretches like a finger into the sea. At its furthest tip stands the Royal Lighthouse.

Waves crash onto the rocks below.
But no boats have ever come to harm.
Every night, the firestone which lights
the lighthouse begins to glow ...
and glow ... until it BLAZES
into the darkness and
saves them.

But one night, just before
dawn, the firestone stopped
glowing. It faded away ...
until there was no light at all,
not even a glimmer.

Lucy, the Royal Lighthouse Keeper's daughter, woke up very early. It was still dark, but there should have been a light shining out to sea. She rushed to the window. No light shone from the lighthouse.

Lucy ran to tell her father.
"The firestone has stopped glowing!"
she cried. "Boats will crash onto the
rocks!"

Her father pulled on his clothes. "We must find another firestone," he said. "But where?"

Lucy took a big box labelled
ROYAL LIGHTHOUSE - RECORDS
AND REPORTS out of the cupboard
and looked through all the papers.

There were records about the weather.

WEATHER RECORD

17 December
Strong east wind —
gales and high seas.
Very cold.

18 December
Stormy seas all day.
Heavy rain just before dark.

19. December
Wind dropped.
Weak sun.
Still cold.

There were reports about visitors.

Saturday 7 June
The King's Summer Visit

The King arrived at 10 a.m.
After inspecting the Royal
Lighthouse, he enjoyed a light
lunch of fresh mackerel with
brown bread and butter.
The King left at 4 p.m.

Everything is very pleasing.
Well done.
Signed : King William

But there was nothing about a
firestone, until, right at the bottom,
Lucy found a scrap of paper, old and
torn. On it was written:

Deep in the dark
the firestones wait,
Where icy east winds blow,

"It's part of a puzzle," said the Royal Lighthouse Keeper.

"I'm off to Windy Bay!" said Lucy, packing her bag. "That's where the east winds blow! Maybe I'll find a firestone there."

"Watch out for the Shifting Sands!" called her father.

"I will!" shouted Lucy.

But she didn't.
When she reached Windy Bay,
there was a sign:

DANGER
Shifting Sands
Wait here for your guides

But Lucy didn't wait. At first the
sand was firm beneath her feet.
But then it became squishy -
and squashy ...

...and very, very squelchy.

Out of the air dropped a flock of
seabirds.
"You should have waited!" screeched
a seagull. "We were on our way to
guide you."

They plucked Lucy out of
the sand and carried her
across to Windy Bay village.

"Thank you," she said as they set her down.

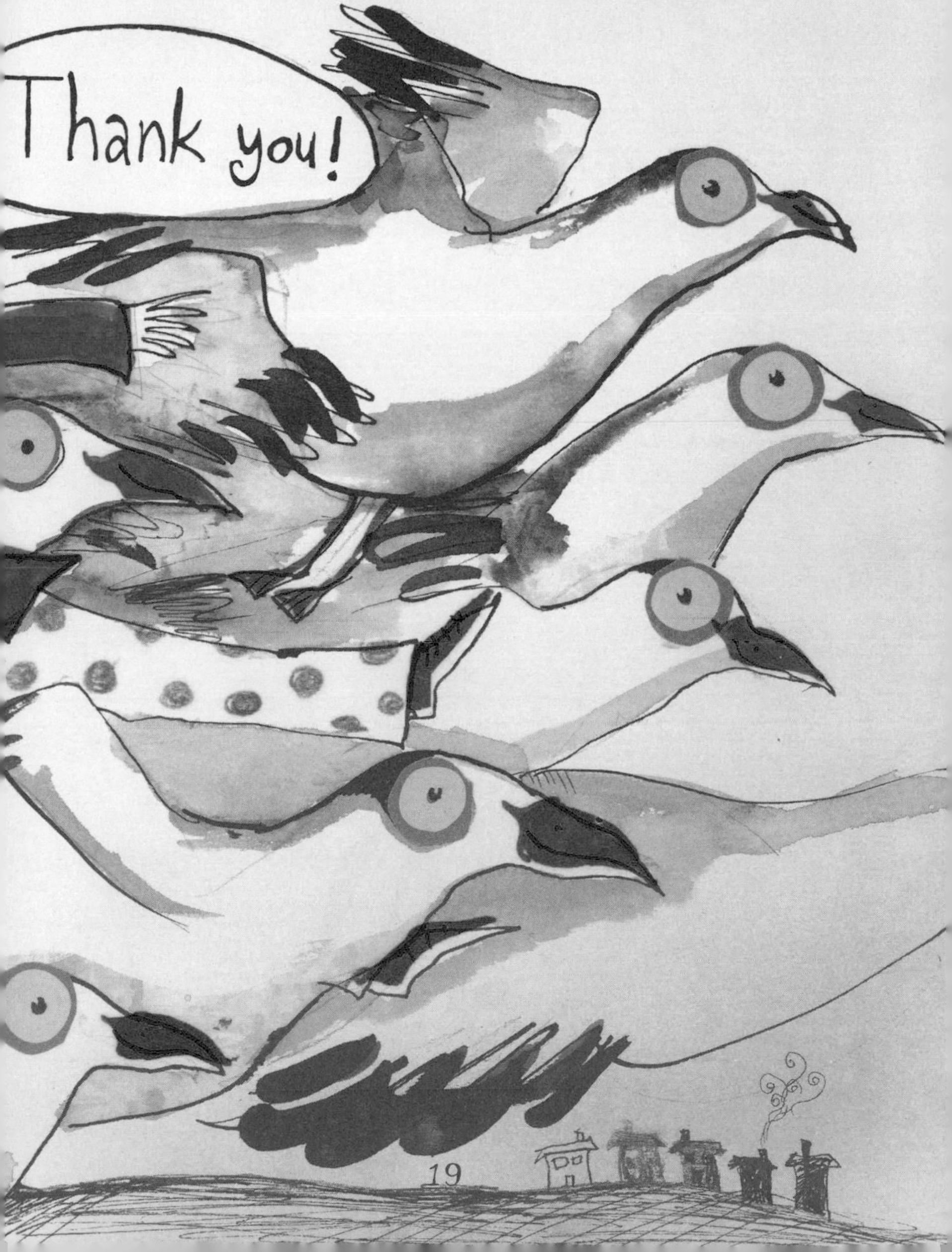

Lucy knocked on every door. No one knew about a firestone, until, at the very last cottage, Lucy met a cheery old woman.

"A firestone? I remember a poem," said the old woman.

20

"I need to find a forest!" cried Lucy.
She pulled a map out of her bag.

"Fir Forest!" said Lucy. "Maybe I'll find a firestone there." She packed up her map and set off at a run.

"Keep to the sorrel path!" called the old woman.

"I will!" shouted Lucy.

But she didn't.
At first, when she reached the forest,
she walked along the sorrel path.
But then she came to a sign:

Cottage Tea
Garden
TEA, ICE CREAM,
LEMONADE

Maybe someone at the tea garden
will know where I can find a
firestone, thought Lucy. So she left
the path and came to the cottage.

25

Outside were lots of tables and chairs.
At one of them sat a dragon, his nose
in a newspaper.
Lucy sat down at an empty table.

At once a big brown bear appeared.
"Can I help you?" he growled.
"Yes, please," she said. "I'm trying
to find a firestone."
"We don't serve firestones," snapped
the bear. "Only what's on the menu.
Iced cake? Chocolate
biscuit?"

"I've heard of a firestone," said a voice behind them. It was the dragon.

"I know you!" cried Lucy. "You're Arthur Scaly-Dragon. You own the Bookshop-on-the-Mountain!"

"At your service," said Arthur. He bowed low. "I've got just the book for you. Let's go!"

Lucy leapt on his back. Arthur rose
into the air. He flew over the forest and
up into the mountains to his cave.

"No time to lose," he agreed
when Lucy told him her
story. "It'll be dark soon."

He gave Lucy a book:
FLINTS AND FIRESTONES.

Lucy turned the pages. There were
firestones of different colours.
There were firestones of different
shapes and sizes. There were pictures
of lighthouses with firestones.

The very last picture was the Royal
Lighthouse itself. Next to it was a poem:

Deep in the dark
the firestones wait,
Where icy east winds blow,
Where tall and strong,
alive with song,
Ancient fir trees grow.
Close to the sea,
in a circle, lie
Firestones to light the sky.

Suddenly Lucy knew where to find
a firestone.
Arthur whisked her down the
mountain and home. Lucy's father
came running out to greet them.

Close to the lighthouse was
a circle of trees. They were
fir trees, bent by the wind
over the years, yet still
alive with birdsong.

"The firestones lie under
the ground!" cried Lucy.
"The book says we need a
spell to raise one."
She opened her book again
and read out loud:

Spell to Raise a Firestone
Spirit of birdsong and of tree,
Spirit of earth and rolling sea,
Give to us as daylight dies
A firestone to light the skies.

At that moment, there was a deep
rumbling in the earth. In front of
them the ground cracked open.

Out of the crack rose ... a firestone!

Everyone gasped.

Quickly, Lucy carried it to the top of the Royal Lighthouse.

Dusk was falling. Waves crashed onto the rocks below. But no boats would come to harm.

As night closed in,
the firestone began
to glow ... and glow
...until it BLAZED
into the darkness.

For Lucy Anna
J.C.
For Polly Lely
P.D.

First published 2004 by Walker Books Ltd
87 Vauxhall Walk, London SE11 5HJ

4 6 8 10 9 7 5 3

Text © 2004 June Crebbin
Illustrations © 2004 Polly Dunbar

This book has been typeset in Alpha Normal, Alpha Bold,
Calligraphic and Sassoon Primary

Handlettering by Polly Dunbar

Printed in China

British Library Cataloguing in Publication Data:
a catalogue record for this book
is available from the British Library

ISBN 978-0-7445-6596-6

www.walkerbooks.co.uk